Emma's First Agate

by Jim Magnuson
Illustrations by Meagan LeMay

Adventure Publications
Cambridge, Minnesota

Dedications

To my grandparents, who always patiently inspired and nurtured my curiosity for the world around me.

—Jim Magnuson

To my parents, who gave me my first sketchbook, even though it may have been to stop me from drawing on the furniture.

—Meagan LeMay

Edited by Ryan Jacobson
Cover and book design by Jonathan Norberg

10 9 8 7 6 5 4 3 2

Copyright 2014 by Jim Magnuson and Meagan LeMay
Published by Adventure Publications
An imprint of AdventureKEEN
820 Cleveland Street South
Cambridge, Minnesota 55008
(800) 678-7006
www.adventurepublications.net
Printed in China
ISBN: 978-1-59193-443-1

Emma's First Agate

Emma loves to be outdoors. She especially likes to collect things. She's always bringing home rocks, flowers and sometimes even turtles or lizards.

Her grandpa is a collector, too. Emma likes to visit him and see his amazing rock collection. She likes to hear stories about when he was a boy.

Grandpa used to roam the fields by his house and along the creek, looking for unique and interesting rocks.

Grandpa smiles when he remembers his rock-hunting adventures, like the stone he found by accident.

"I was rock hunting with my dad," says Grandpa. "I got tired and sat in the shade of a tree. I noticed a colorful stone, so I started shouting. My dad thought something was wrong. But when I showed him the rock, he just shook his head."

"Do you still have that rock?" asks Emma. "Will you show it to me?"

Grandpa goes to his treasure collection. He digs around until he finds what he's looking for. He loves to show off his favorite gem.

"Wow, it's beautiful," says Emma. "What kind of rock is that?"

Grandpa answers, "This is an agate. Agates are very rare. You usually have to look really hard to find one."

As her curiosity grows, Emma picks up interesting rocks everywhere. It drives her brother and sister crazy.

Mom worries about Emma's growing rock collection. She tries to get rid of a few stones without Emma noticing. But Emma does notice.

"Mom, have you seen my black rock with the red speckles? It was here yesterday!"

Summer finally arrives, and Emma is excited about the family trip to the lake.

Everyone else gathers their sand pails and shovels, towels and swimwear. But Emma only brings a bucket for collecting rocks.

At the beach, Emma's brother and sister build a sand castle, but Emma has no interest in that. She walks up and down the shoreline, looking at all the stones.

Emma searches all afternoon, but she does not find an agate.

Soon, her mother calls, "Emma, we'll be leaving in five minutes."

Emma feels more worried than ever. She wants to find an agate, but she's almost out of time.

Suddenly, Emma spots something. There, in the shallow water, she sees a red-and-white-striped stone with small dimples. It looks just like the one Grandpa has!

Emma dashes into the lake. A wave splashes against her as she picks up her prize.

Emma runs straight to her Grandpa, holding out the stone and calling, "Grandpa, look what I found!"

Grandpa scoops up Emma and squeezes her in a bear hug. "You've made me so proud. You didn't give up, and you found an agate! Now you have your own story to tell."

Rock hounding and agate hunting are wonderful learning experiences for children. They are hobbies that provide endless hours of enjoyment, and seeking out treasures isn't the only fun. Sorting, displaying and learning about the stones are great pastimes, too. Like any hobby, it's great to have a little information to get started. The chart below is meant to give you a quick idea about some of the most popular agates in the continental United States. *Imagine how big your child's eyes will be when they find their first agate!*

Lake Superior Agate
Found in the Upper Midwest from the north shore of Lake Superior all the way to Iowa; popular hunting locations are lakes, rivers, creeks, farm fields and gravel pits. **Characteristics:** Beautiful banding patterns with many color combinations; red and white stones are sometimes called "candy stripes." Other colors include gray, black and white, and "painted agates" with colors that include bright orange, blue, yellow, green, pink and lavender.

Fairburn Agate
Found in the South Dakota grasslands between the Black Hills and the Badlands. **Characteristics:** Beautiful banding patterns that some say are like a holly leaf with sharply pointed ends. Fairburns can contain a rainbow of colors in a single stone, though caramel, rose, black and white combinations are the most common.

Prairie Agate/Picture Rock
Found in the South Dakota grasslands between the Black Hills and the Badlands. **Characteristics:** Wavy banding patterns with varying color schemes; stones with caramel, white and some rose colors are most common; those with black and white combinations are often the most beautiful.

Bubblegum Agate
Found in the South Dakota grasslands between the Black Hills and the Badlands. **Characteristics:** Small sizes ranging from marble to almost golf-ball with bubbly surfaces that look like a ball of chewed gum—usually showing pinkish and black colors on the outside. When cut open, Bubblegum Agates reveal white, yellow, pink and rose color bands.

Teepee Canyon Agate
Found in South Dakota near the southern end of the Black Hills in Teepee Canyon near the town of Custer. **Characteristics:** Tan-colored stones that can be as large as a softball. When broken open, Teepee Canyon Agates show beautiful and very bright color bands including reds, oranges, yellows, purples, pinks and whites.

Montana Moss Agate
Found in southeastern Montana in stream beds and gravel bars along the Yellowstone River; also found in northern Wyoming and western portions of the Dakotas. **Characteristics:** Montana Moss Agates need to be cut to enjoy their beauty. Inside these agates you will find patterns that resemble natural landscapes or that have banding patterns with beautiful bluish or dark brown color combinations.

Crowley's Ridge Agate
Found in southeastern Missouri and northeastern Arkansas in sand and gravel deposits near a Mississippi River formation known as Crowley's Ridge. **Characteristics:** Crowley's Ridge Agates have banding patterns similar to Lake Superior Agates. Reddish colorations are common with some beautiful pink or lavender tones mixed in. They also come in pale yellow and tan color combinations.

Montana Dryhead Agate
Found near the Bighorn Canyon National Recreation Area of southern Montana and northern Wyoming. **Characteristics:** Dryhead agates have intense banding patterns with striking color combinations, most notably bright oranges, whites, pinks and yellows. These agates are usually set within a dark-chocolate-colored stone that makes the agate pattern all the more beautiful.

Fire Agate
Found in the southwestern deserts of the U.S., especially in areas near the Colorado River, near Needles, CA, and Kingman, AZ. **Characteristics:** Fire Agate is a truly unique and highly prized form of agate. These stones show glowing rainbow colorations with a bubbly outer surface. What these agates lack in size they make up for with beauty and dazzling colors.

Carnelian Agate
Found on the western foothills of the Cascade Mountains between Eugene, OR, and Olympia, WA. **Characteristics:** Carnelian Agates have soft and wavy banding patterns that are set within amber-yellow to orange-colored stone that glows beautifully when light passes through it.

Baker Ranch Thunder Egg Agate
Found in far southwestern New Mexico near the town of Deming at the Baker Ranch Mine. **Characteristics:** Baker Ranch Thunder Egg Agates contain both banding patterns and "starburst" formations with a range of colors including pink, blue, gray, white, red and black. These agates are strongly fluorescent and will glow bright green and red under shortwave ultraviolet light!

About the Author

Growing up in rural Illinois, Jim Magnuson spent much of his free time in the woods and fields hunting for wild nuts, berries and mushrooms, and also for fossils that were abundant in the limestone quarries and in creek beds. Of all these treasures from the earth, the fossils were his true passion; he would often come home, his pockets bulging with his latest finds. His mother lovingly referred to Jim as "Mr. Got Rocks." Now Jim spends much of his free time in gravel pits, farm fields and other outdoor locales where there are accumulations of Lake Superior gravel. He loves to share his hobby with family and friends. The earth is full of many treasures, and Jim is always able to find peace through hunting, polishing and organizing for presentation, and giving away agates to those who find them interesting and beautiful.

About the Illustrator

Meagan LeMay has been drawing since she was old enough to hold a pencil. Although her only formal art education is in sculpture and history, drawing and painting are her preferred mediums. Meagan grew up in Minnesota, but her influences mostly stem from the eastern hemisphere. She has studied both the Japanese and Chinese languages and draws inspiration from both cultures. She hopes to continue growing as an artist.